THE COUNTRY MOUSE
AND THE
CITY MOUSE

Illustrated by Laura Lydecker

ALFRED A. KNOPF, NEW YORK

This is a Borzoi Book
published by Alfred A. Knopf, Inc.

Illustrations copyright © 1987 by Laura Lydecker
All rights reserved under International and Pan-American Copyright Conventions.
Published in the United States by Alfred A. Knopf, Inc., New York, and simultaneously in Canada by
Random House of Canada Limited, Toronto. Distributed by Random House, Inc., New York.
Manufactured in Singapore 10 9 8 7 6 5 4 3 2 1

Library of Congress Cataloging-in-Publication Data
Country mouse and the city mouse. English. The country mouse and the city mouse.
Summary: When the city mouse and the country mouse visit each
other, they decide they prefer their own way of living.
[1. Fables] I. Lydecker, Laura, ill. II. Title. PZ8.2.A255Co 1987 398.2′45293233
[E] 86-27238 ISBN 0-394-89027-2
ISBN 0-394-99027-7 (lib. bdg.)

The version of *The Country Mouse and the City Mouse* used in this
book is based most closely on the one found in Sir Roger L'Estrange's *Fables
of Aesop and Other Mythologists,* first published in 1692.

For my beloved mother,
to whom I owe everything

Once upon a time a Country Mouse invited her friend from the city to share a simple country supper with her.

The Country Mouse brought out every morsel of her rough country food and set it all on the table—crusts of moldy bread, bowls of musty oatmeal, and crumbs of dried cheese and bacon.

The City Mouse was very polite, so she pretended to enjoy the humble meal and took many helpings.

But after eating all she could, she exclaimed, "My friend, why do you lead such a lonesome, starving life as this? Why are you miserable when you could be happy? If you would only come to town with me, you could have everything your heart desires."

The Country Mouse could not resist the City Mouse's tempting invitation. So the two friends set out together that very evening, and by midnight they had reached the great house in town where the City Mouse lived.

Scampering from room to room, the City Mouse showed her friend the larder, the pantry, and the kitchen, and in each room she said, "This is where I store my food."

Then she led the Country Mouse into the grand dining room. On the table they found the leftovers from a splendid banquet, for there had been a party that very night.

The Country Mouse was tired and hungry from the long journey, so she sat upon a velvet couch, and the City Mouse served her delicate cakes and pastries, fine cheeses and nuts, and sparkling champagne.

The poor country bumpkin had never eaten so
grandly, and as she nibbled she thought, "How lucky I
am to have left my hole in the country for such a rich
and exciting place as this."

But just then, the door flew open . . .

. . . and in burst a crowd of roaring bullies, returning from a late party with their barking dogs.

"Run for your life!" the City Mouse cried, and she disappeared so quickly, her friend could not tell where she had gone.

The Country Mouse looked frantically about for a place to hide, but she was so new to this sport and so frightened that she could barely move.

At last she slipped into a dark corner, where she lay trembling and panting until the noisy crowd had gone.

As soon as the house was quiet again, the Country Mouse decided to say good-bye to her city friend.

She stole out from her hiding place and whispered to the City Mouse: "I'm sorry but I don't much like your city adventures. If this is how you live, I'll go back to my cottage and my moldy cheese. I would much rather stay in my hole nibbling crusts without danger than feast like a queen in fear of my life."